Monster Molly's BIG Day Out

By Dee Reid

RUby Tuesday Books

Tips for Reading Together

- Set aside about 10 minutes each day for reading.
- Find a quiet place to sit with no distractions. Turn off the TV, music and screens.
- Encourage the child to hold the book and turn the pages.
- Before reading begins, look at the pictures together and talk about what you see.
- If the child gets stuck on a word, ask them what sound the first letter makes. Then, you read to the end of the sentence. Often by knowing the first sound and hearing the rest of the sentence, the child will be able to figure out the unknown word. Looking at the pictures can help, too.

Above all enjoy the time together and make reading fun!

Book Band Yellow

www.rubytuesdaybooks.com

Molly was sad.

5

Let's go to the park.

I am happy!

Molly sat in the bus.

Max sat on the bus.

It is cold on the bus.

Max walked into the park.

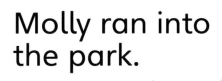

Molly ran into the park.

Max went down on the see-saw.

Molly went on the little swing.

Max went on the big swing.

Max went in a big puddle.

Can you find the opposites?

happy

hot

wet

little

up

big

cold

dry

sad

down

Can you remember?

Who was sad?

How did Molly and Max get to the park?

Who sat on the bus?

Who went on the big swing?

Why did Molly laugh at Max?

Can you read these words?

big   is   on

the   was   went